On a Plane

Roderick Hunt • Annemarie Young

Alex Brychta

OXFORD

UNIVERSITY PRESS

"Hooray!" yelled Dad. "We've won a holiday in the Canary Islands. We'll fly out and stay in a four star hotel near the beach."

4

"We've never been on a plane before," said Biff.

"Or stayed in a hotel," said Chip.

"I can't wait!" said Kipper.

"Thanks, Floppy!" said Dad. "The
competition was on your dog food
packet and we won."

"Good old Floppy," said Biff.

"We'll go at half term," said Mum.
"We can't take Floppy with us, but
Gran will look after him."

"He'll like that," said Chip.

At last it was time to pack.

Biff had too many clothes. "You don't need that many," said Mum.

Kipper had too many toys. "You can't take all of those," said Dad.

Chip got it right. "T-shirt, shorts, a hat and a book," he said.

They went to the airport on a
coach ...

... they had to wait to check in ...

... they handed over their bags ...

... they showed their passports.
Kipper had made one for Ted.

They went through security.
Kipper's bag had to go through an
X-ray machine – and so did Teddy.
  "Don't get lost, Ted," said Kipper.

At last it was time to board the plane. Kipper was excited. The plane was really big.

"This plane is massive," said
Kipper. "It has so many seats."
"These are ours," said Mum.
Everyone wanted the window seat.

In the end, they let Kipper sit by
the window.

"Get your books and games, and
settle down quickly," said Dad.

The flight attendant was called
Guy. He gave the children a pack of
things to do.

"It's a long flight," said Guy.

"Fasten your seatbelts and make
sure the seat is upright," said Guy.
Then he told everyone what to do in
case of an emergency.

"Will you hold my hand when we take off?" said Mum. "I get scared."

"All right," said Kipper. "I'm not scared. It's exciting."

After a while, the flight attendants
gave out food on little trays.

"I'm not very hungry," said Biff.

"Well I am," said Dad.

At last the plane landed. "That wasn't so bad," said Mum.

Their passports were checked.

They got their bags. "Now to find our hotel," said Dad.

They saw a minibus. "This one will take us to the hotel," said Dad.

The minibus driver stopped at a
hotel. "Here is your hotel," he said.
"Oh no!" said Mum.

The hotel looked terrible. It was
old and dirty.

"Look!" said Kipper. "This isn't
our hotel. The picture is different."

"Kipper is right," said Dad. "This
is the wrong hotel!"

Just then a taxi came along. Mum
waved and it stopped.

Mum asked the driver if she could take them. She showed her the address of their hotel.

"Get in," said the driver.

"This is better," said Mum.

"Well done, Kipper!" said Dad.

"This is going to be a great holiday, after all."

Talk about the story

Why was everyone pleased with Floppy?

What did the family do before they got on the plane?

How did Kipper know they were at the wrong hotel?

How would you most like to travel on holiday?

What would *you* take on holiday?

Which of these things do you think Kipper took on holiday?
Which ones can you find in the pictures of the story?

What would you take on holiday?

Teddy

Wellington boots

sunscreen

passport

camera

Floppy

watering can

umbrella

hat

book

t-shirt

Find the right minibus

Which minibus has this picture on it?